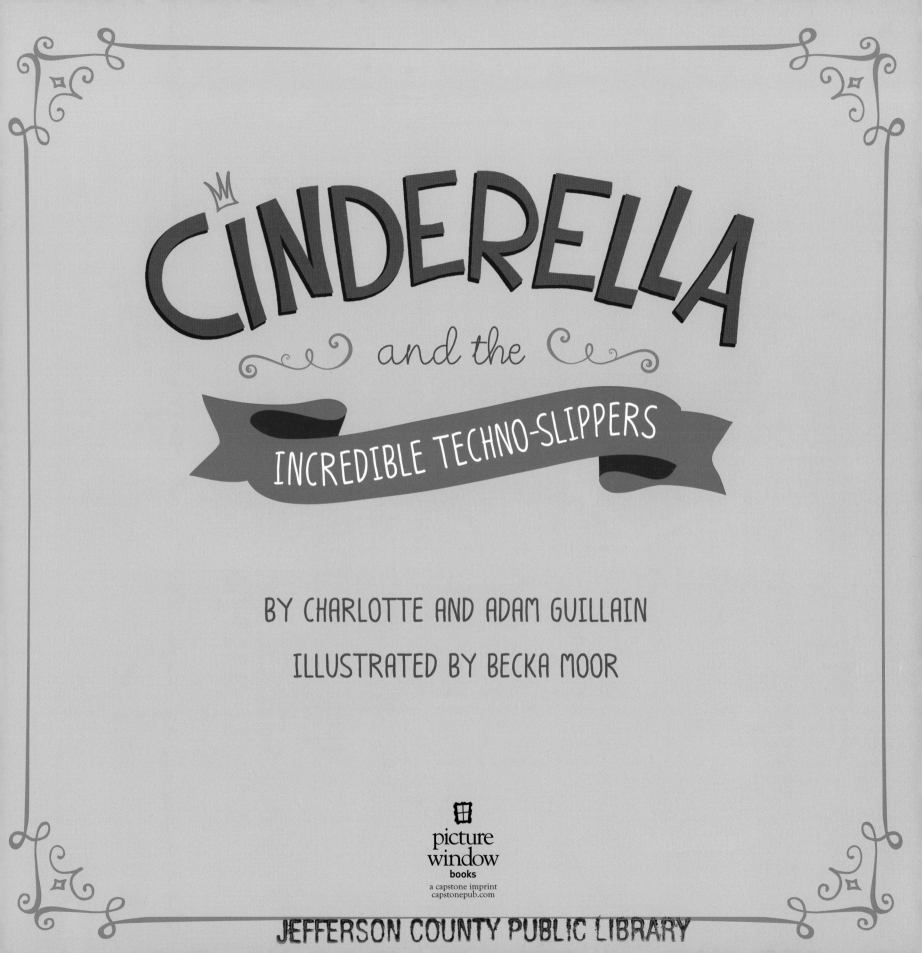

CINDERELLA and the

INCREDIBLE TECHNO-SLIPPERS

BY CHARLOTTE AND ADAM GUILLAIN

ILLUSTRATED BY BECKA MOOR

picture
window
books

a capstone imprint
capstonepub.com

This story is based on the fairy tale Cinderella. There are several versions of the story including ones from Jacob Grimm (1785–1863) and Wilhelm Grimm (1786–1859), Charles Perrault (1628–1703), and Giambattista Basile (1566–1632).

Perhaps the most famous version is as follows. A girl's mother dies and her father remarries. His new wife has two daughters who make the girl work in the kitchen and call her Cinderella, because she is always dirty from the ashes from the fire. When her stepsisters are invited to a royal ball, Cinderella is told she can't go. However, she is helped by a fairy godmother and goes to the ball, where nobody recognizes her. She dances with the prince, but leaves a slipper behind as she runs away at the end. The prince takes the slipper to find Cinderella. In some versions of the tale, it is the birds that show him the way. The slipper fits and the two of them live happily ever after at the palace.

Cinderella and the Incredible Techno-Slippers is published by Picture Window Books
A Capstone Imprint
1710 Roe Crest Drive
North Mankato, Minnesota 56003
www.capstonepub.com

Text copyright © Charlotte and Adam Guillain 2015
Illustrations by Becka Moor

Library of Congress Cataloging-in-Publication Data
Cataloging-in-publication information is on file with the Library of Congress.
ISBN 978-1-4795-8616-5 (hardback)
ISBN 978-1-4795-8754-4 (paperback)
ISBN 978-1-4795-8750-6 (paper-over-board)
ISBN 978-1-4795-8758-2 (ebook)

Editor: James Benefield
Designer: Richard Parker

Printed and bound in the United States of America by Corporate Graphics

CAST OF CHARACTERS

CINDERELLA

CINDERELLA'S DAD

CINDERELLA'S STEPMOTHER

TOBY AND TARA, THE STEPMOTHER'S TWINS

THE TOY FACTORY OWNER

Cinderella and her dad lived happily in a very tall building. From their window they could see the toy factory on the other side of town, where Cinderella's dad worked as an inventor.

BUT THEN EVERYTHING CHANGED.

Cinderella's dad got married, and his new wife moved in, along with her twins, Toby and Tara.

While Cinderella's dad was out at the factory, her new stepmother did **NOTHING.** She never cleaned or even put things in the trash. Instead she made Cinderella do all the work.

CINDERELLA, CLEAN THIS HORRIBLE MESS UP.

The twins made a lot of mess. They were always breaking their toys and expected Cinderella to clean everything up.

Cinderella hid the broken toys under the stairs, where she had an inventing workshop. Using the broken toys, she built an army of robots to clean up for her, so she could spend more time working on her latest invention...

A PAIR OF INCREDIBLE TECHNO-SLIPPERS.

Cinderella loved to dance. The techno slippers made her feet move *perfectly*. With the slippers on, she would **AMAZE** everyone who saw her on a dance floor.

Then, one day, Cinderella's dad came home looking *sad*.

"The toy factory is shutting down!" he said. "I've brought invitations to the goodbye party."

After dinner, Cinderella's dad went back to the factory.
He wanted to clean out his workshop before the party.

Then Cinderella had an **IDEA.**

*The party will be the perfect place to
try out my techno-slippers!* she thought.
That will make Dad smile!

At eight o' clock, it was time for the party.
But Cinderella's stepmother had other plans.

"You must stay here and clean up while we're out!" she screeched.
"We'll be back just after midnight!"

And then the twins and the stepmother left.

Just then, one of
Cinderella's robots
slid into the room.

"One of the invitations!"
cried Cinderella, as the robot
placed a card in her hands.

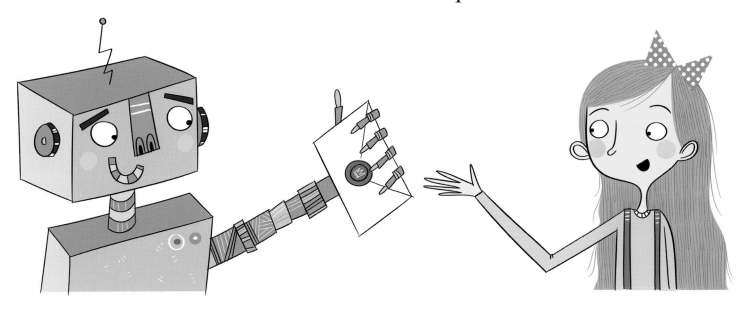

She put on her best dress
and the techno-slippers and set off on her
HOMEMADE SKATEBOARD.

Cinderella arrived at the toy factory just as the party was starting.
Her stepmother and the twins were too busy eating cake and ice
cream to notice she was there. Her dad was busy cleaning
up his things from his old workshop.

Cinderella turned on her techno slippers and hit the dance floor. Everyone **GASPED** as she *twirled* and *whirled!*

HER TECHNO-SLIPPERS WORKED PERFECTLY...

CINDERELLA WAS THE BEST DANCER AT THE PARTY!

"WOW, WHAT AN AMAZING INVENTION!"

exclaimed the factory owner, when he saw the mysterious girl dancing. He was about to ask her about the incredible slippers when the clock struck **MIDNIGHT.**

OH NO! I HAVE TO GET HOME BEFORE THE OTHERS!

But as Cinderella ran out of the door, one of her techno-slippers *fell off*.

The next day, the owner of the toy factory was on television, standing outside the factory. He was holding up Cinderella's missing slipper!

"We will visit every house and apartment in town until we find the owner of this slipper," he said.

"THIS TECHNO SLIPPER IS AN AMAZING INVENTION. IT MIGHT EVEN SAVE THE FACTORY. WE SHOULD GIVE THE INVENTOR A JOB!"

When the owner of the toy factory
finally got to Cinderella's apartment,
her stepmother and Tara fought to try
on the slipper.

Then the factory owner spotted Cinderella.

"What about you?"

he asked.

Cinderella carefully put on both slippers and began to *dance*. The factory owner couldn't believe it. He'd found the inventor of the

Incredible Techno-Slippers!

So Cinderella's dad went back
to work at the factory, and
Cinderella joined him
on weekends.

She invented new toys
happily ever after.
And Cinderella's
stepmother and the twins
had to learn to clean up
after themselves.

11·15